# Mice

Lori Dittmer

seedlings

CREATIVE EDUCATION • CREATIVE PAPERBACKS

Published by Creative Education and Creative Paperbacks
P.O. Box 227, Mankato, Minnesota 56002
Creative Education and Creative Paperbacks are imprints of
The Creative Company
www.thecreativecompany.us

Design by Ellen Huber; production by Dana Cheit
Art direction by Rita Marshall
Printed in the United States of America

Photographs by Dreamstime (Anyaivanova, Fifoprod), iStockphoto (anyaivanova, bloodua, bozhdb, bridge99, CreativeNature_nl, DamianKuzdak, faslooff, GlobalP, hardeko, irin717, JamesBrey, JoeZellner, maxximmm, Pakhnyushchyy, rdegrie, Kuttelvaserova Stuchelova, timnewman), Shutterstock (IrinaK, Szasz-Fabian Jozsef)



Library of Congress Cataloging-in-Publication Data
Names: Dittmer, Lori, author.
Title: Mice / Lori Dittmer.
Series: Seedlings: Backyard Animals.
Includes bibliographical references and index.
Summary: A kindergarten-level introduction to mice, covering their growth process, behaviors, the backyard habitats they call home, and such defining features as their hairless tails.
Identifiers: LCCN 2017051389 / ISBN 978-1-60818-972-4 (hardcover) / ISBN 978-1-62832-599-7 (pbk) / ISBN 978-1-64000-073-5 (eBook)

Subjects: LCSH: Mice—Juvenile literature.
Classification: LCC QL737.R6 D58 2018 / DDC 599.35/3—dc23

CCSS: RI.K.1, 2, 3, 4, 5, 6, 7; RI.1.1, 2, 3, 4, 5, 6, 7; RF.K.1, 3; RF.1.1

First Edition HC 9 8 7 6 5 4 3 2 1
First Edition PBK 9 8 7 6 5 4 3 2 1

# TABLE OF CONTENTS

# Hello, mice!

Small mice are **rodents**.

They live in fields, forests, and backyards.

Many sneak into houses.

Furry mice have long tails.

The tails do not have hair.

Sharp teeth help mice **gnaw** through wood.

Mice are usually brown or gray.

Some are white.

They live in family groups.

Mice like to eat seeds and fruit.

But they will nibble almost anything.

Baby mice are
called pinkies.

They grow fur a few
days after birth.

Mice are ready to have their own babies in about two months.

Tired mice sleep a lot.

They chew holes.

They squeeze through tiny spaces.

# Goodbye, mice!

# Picture a Mouse

ears
whiskers
toes

## Words to Know

**gnaw:** to bite or nibble at something

**rodents:** small, furry animals whose front teeth never stop growing

## Read More

Riggs, Kate. *Mice.*
Mankato, Minn.: Creative Education, 2017.

Schuetz, Kari. *Mice.*
Minneapolis: Bellwether Media, 2014.

## Websites

Pest World for Kids: Mice
http://pestworldforkids.org/pest-guide/mice/
Learn more about mice, including what they eat and where thcy live.

Science Kids: Fun Mouse Facts for Kids
http://www.sciencekids.co.nz/sciencefacts/animals/mouse.html
Read more fun facts about mice.

**Note:** Every effort has been made to ensure that the websites listed above are suitable for children, that they have educational value, and that they contain no inappropriate material. However, because of the nature of the Internet, it is impossible to guarantee that these sites will remain active indefinitely or that their contents will not be altered.

# Index